This
Sprog Owner's Manual
belongs to

. . . .

The Sprog Owner's MANUAL

WARNING NOTE

Before acquiring a
sprog, please read the
following instructions

VERY CAREFULLY

The Sprog Owner's Manual

Babette Cole

Red Fox

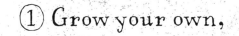

① Grow your own,

② adopt a ready-made one,

a Sprog

③ 'Rent-a-Sprog'

or ④ send off for one from a mail-order catalogue.

How to Recognise
a Good Sprog

Curly, shiny hair

Shell-like ears

Sunny smile

Good teeth

Nice smell of soap

No need for defence
mechanism

Bodywork
in good
condition

Kind to
animals

Pleasant
outlook

Dainty feet

How to Recognise
a Bad Sprog

Piggy eyes

Eyebrows meet

Sticky hair

Spiky ears

Nasty grin

Fangs

Horrible pong

Bodywork in
bad condition
(smell of
rotten eggs)

Unpleasant
outlook

Defence
mechanism

Big smelly feet

(Animals are frightened
of this kind of sprog)

Fuel (or What Sprogs Eat)

Good sprog fuel (healthy)

Bad sprog fuel
(unhealthy)

Fuel Processing for Body

Inside the good sprog

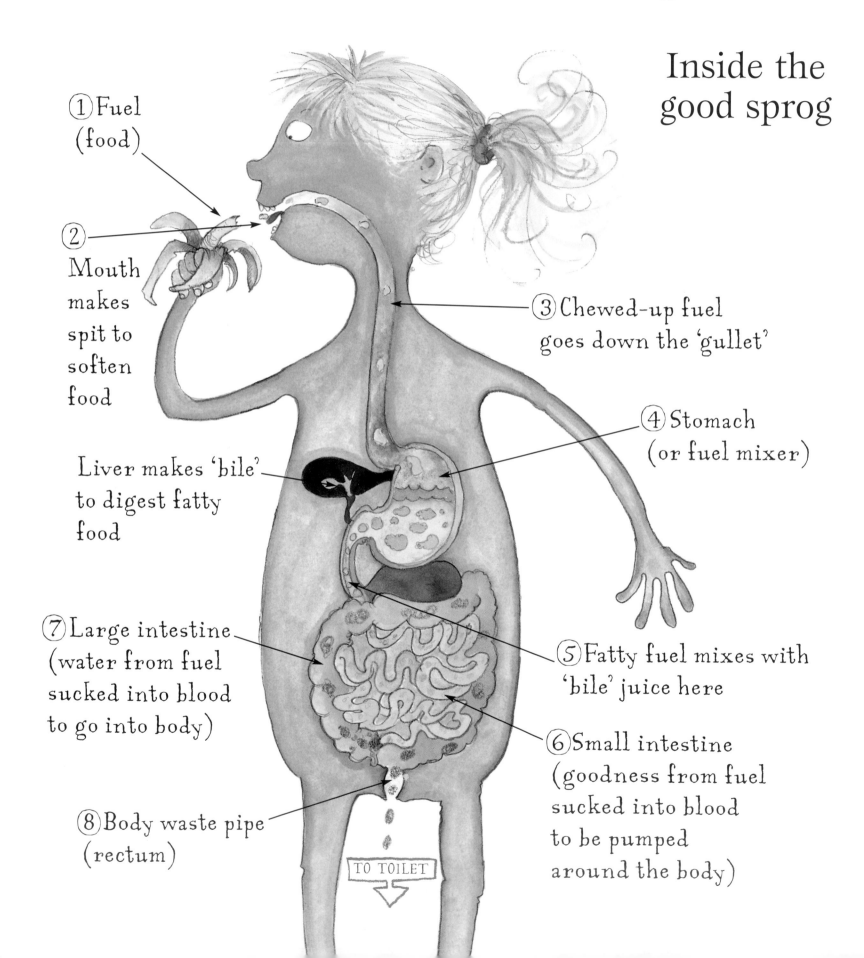

① Fuel (food)

② Mouth makes spit to soften food

③ Chewed-up fuel goes down the 'gullet'

④ Stomach (or fuel mixer)

Liver makes 'bile' to digest fatty food

⑤ Fatty fuel mixes with 'bile' juice here

⑥ Small intestine (goodness from fuel sucked into blood to be pumped around the body)

⑦ Large intestine (water from fuel sucked into blood to go into body)

⑧ Body waste pipe (rectum)

TO TOILET

Performance (or Digestion)

Inside the bad sprog

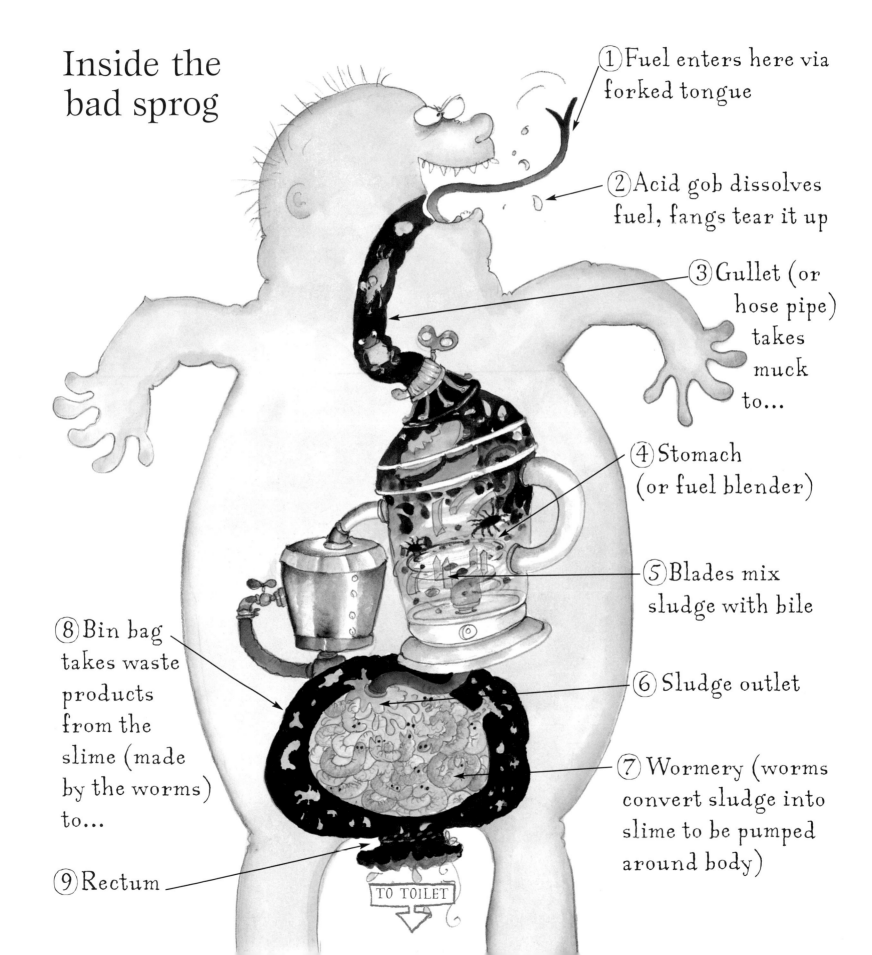

① Fuel enters here via forked tongue

② Acid gob dissolves fuel, fangs tear it up

③ Gullet (or hose pipe) takes muck to...

④ Stomach (or fuel blender)

⑤ Blades mix sludge with bile

⑥ Sludge outlet

⑦ Wormery (worms convert sludge into slime to be pumped around body)

⑧ Bin bag takes waste products from the slime (made by the worms) to...

⑨ Rectum

TO TOILET

Waste Disposal
(or Potty Training)

Disposal unit (or 'nappy')

Normal amount of disposable waste for a good baby sprog

Normal position for waste disposal in good toddler sprog

GOOD SPROG

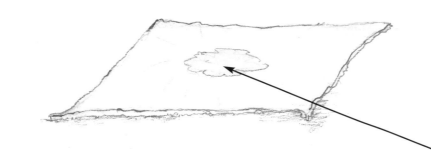

Disposal unit (or 'potty')

Normal position for waste disposal in good older sprog

Disposal unit (or 'toilet')

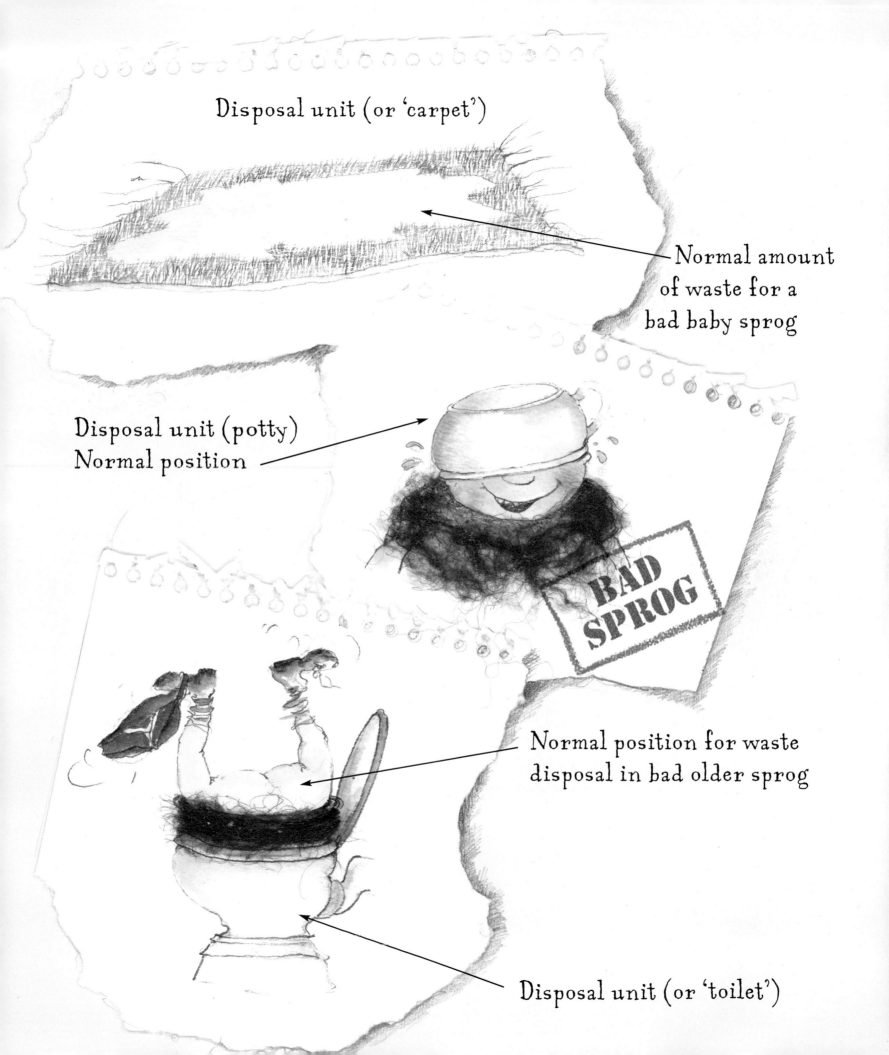

Disposal unit (or 'carpet')

Normal amount of waste for a bad baby sprog

Disposal unit (potty) Normal position

BAD SPROG

Normal position for waste disposal in bad older sprog

Disposal unit (or 'toilet')

Air Intake (Breathing Equipment)

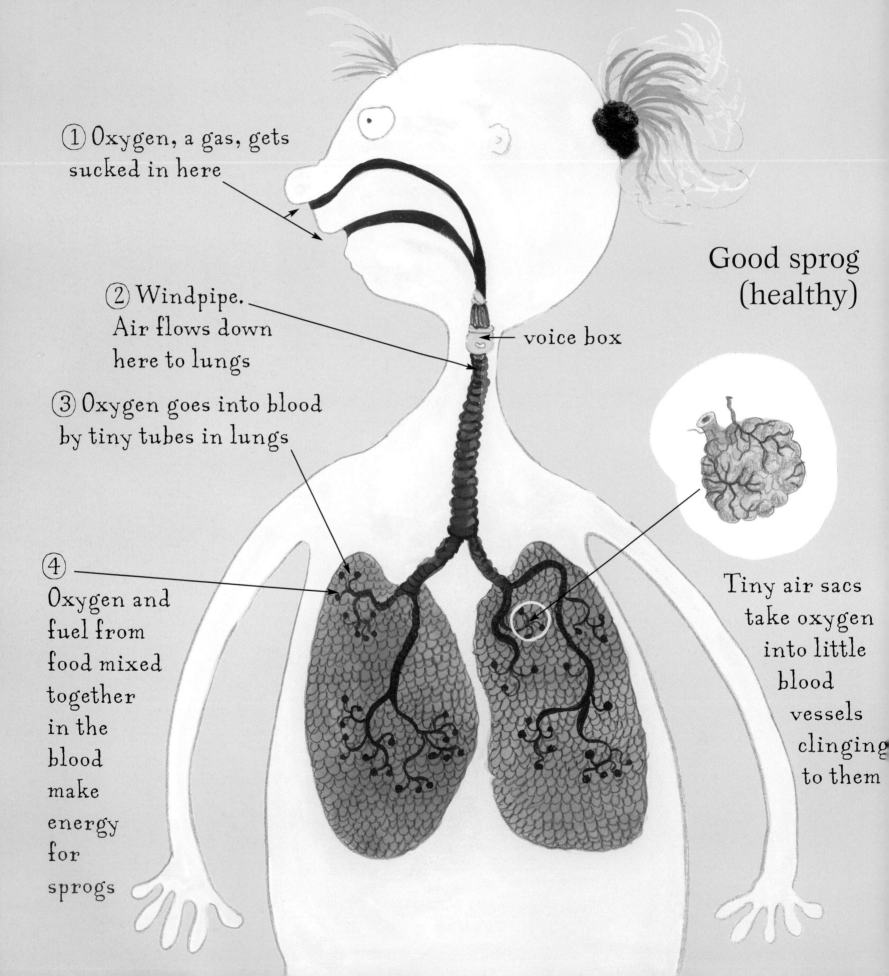

① Oxygen, a gas, gets sucked in here

② Windpipe. Air flows down here to lungs

③ Oxygen goes into blood by tiny tubes in lungs

④ Oxygen and fuel from food mixed together in the blood make energy for sprogs

voice box

Good sprog (healthy)

Tiny air sacs take oxygen into little blood vessels clinging to them

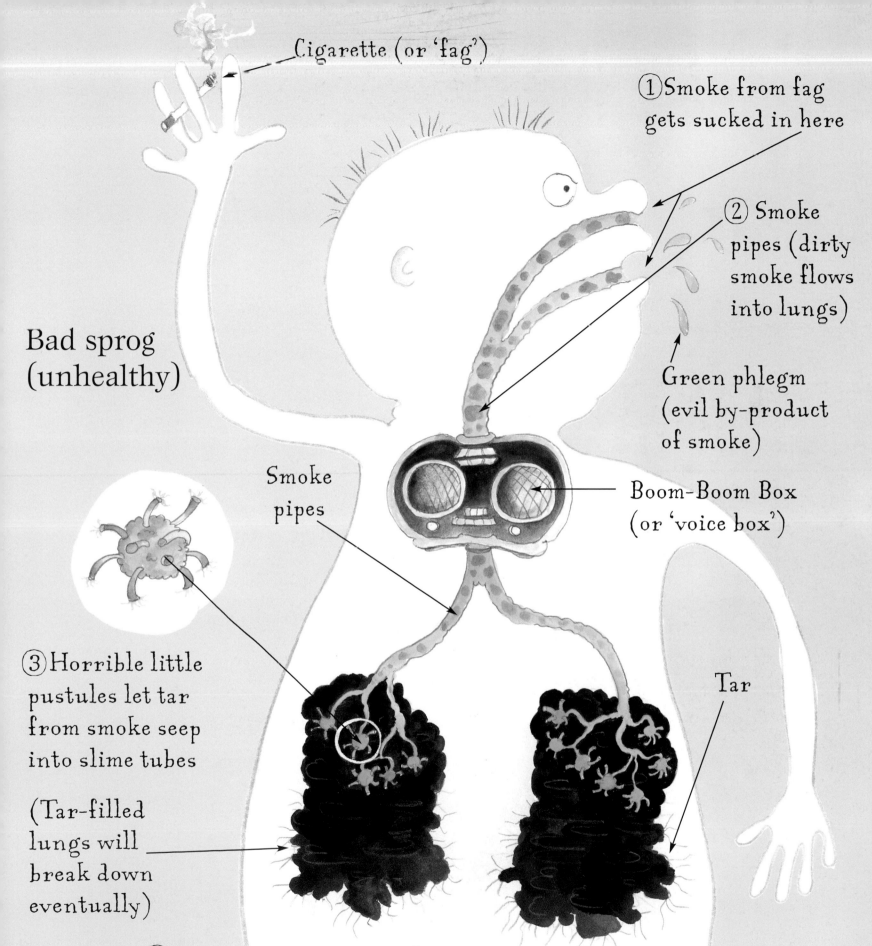

Sprog Pumping System

Good sprogs have BLOOD, a liquid that takes fuel and oxygen to all parts of the body to give energy. A good sprog has around five litres of it.

Tubes that take blood away from the heart are called arteries. They are bright red because they are full of oxygen

Tubes which take blood to the heart are called veins. They are dark purple because the oxygen in the blood has been used up

Heart or pump that keeps blood moving in thin tubes around the body

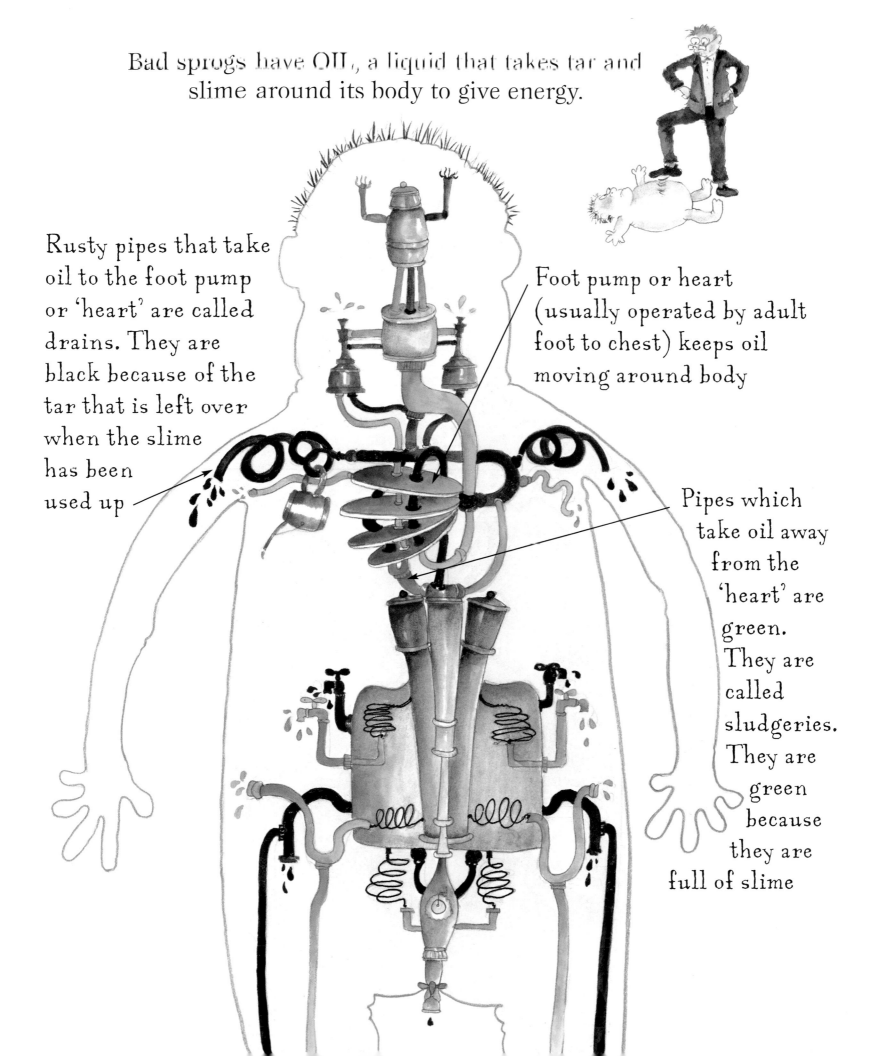

Bad sprogs have OIL, a liquid that takes tar and slime around its body to give energy.

Rusty pipes that take oil to the foot pump or 'heart' are called drains. They are black because of the tar that is left over when the slime has been used up

Foot pump or heart (usually operated by adult foot to chest) keeps oil moving around body

Pipes which take oil away from the 'heart' are green. They are called sludgeries. They are green because they are full of slime

Framework and Fittings

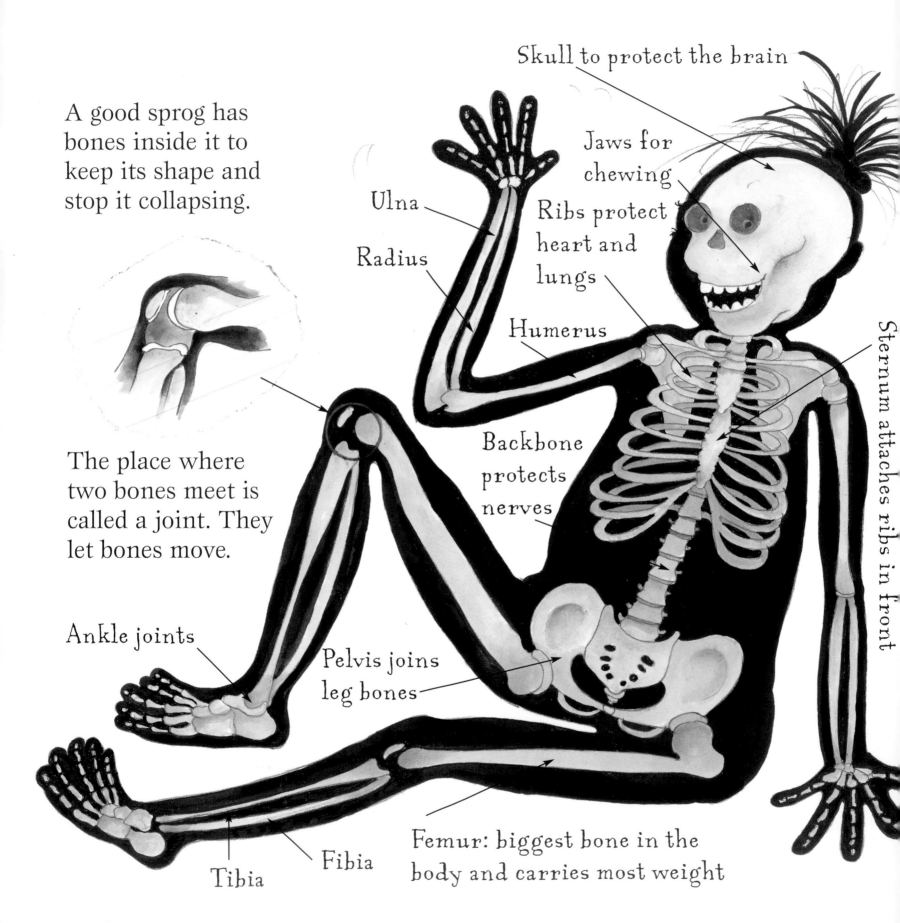

A good sprog has bones inside it to keep its shape and stop it collapsing.

The place where two bones meet is called a joint. They let bones move.

Ankle joints

Skull to protect the brain

Jaws for chewing

Ribs protect heart and lungs

Ulna

Radius

Humerus

Backbone protects nerves

Sternum attaches ribs in front

Pelvis joins leg bones

Femur: biggest bone in the body and carries most weight

Tibia

Fibia

(or How Sprogs Move)

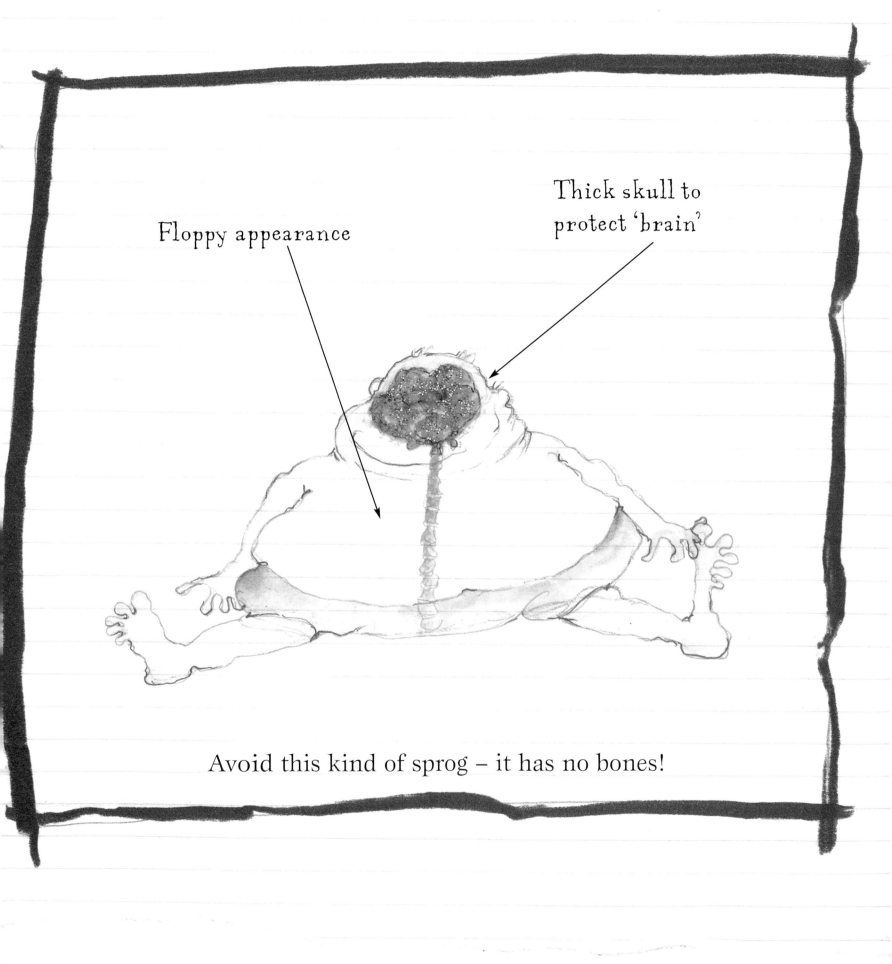

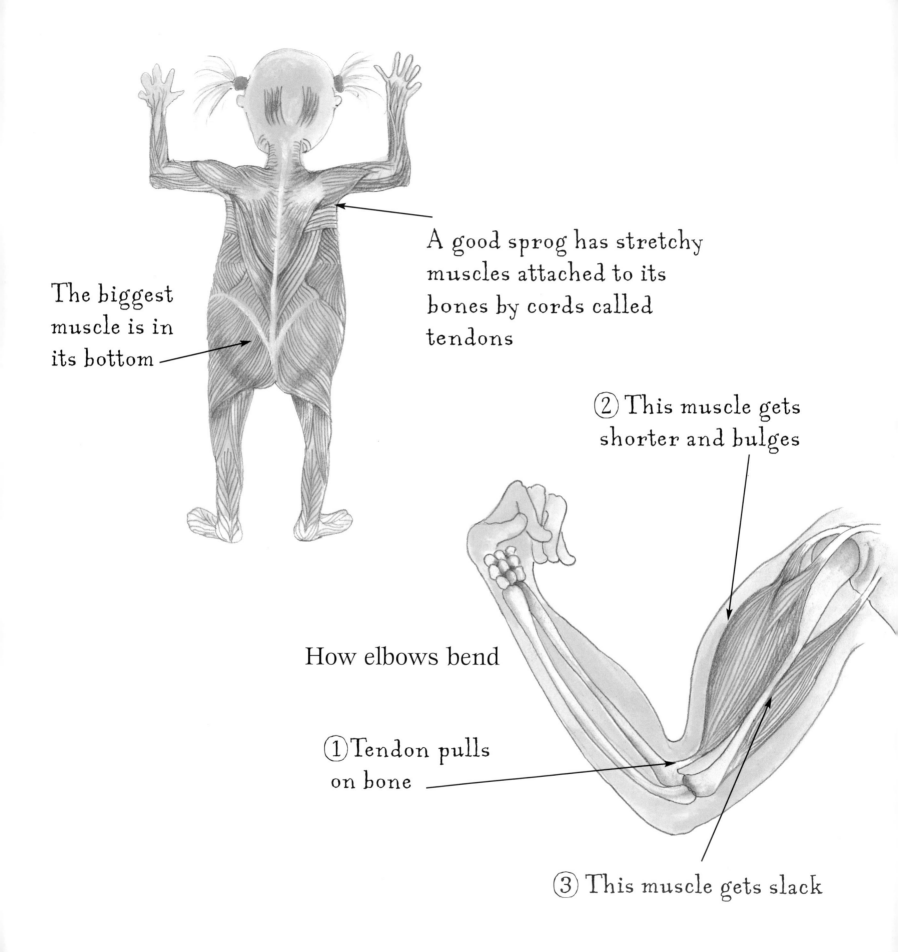

The biggest muscle is in its bottom

A good sprog has stretchy muscles attached to its bones by cords called tendons

② This muscle gets shorter and bulges

How elbows bend

① Tendon pulls on bone

③ This muscle gets slack

How Sprogs Move, continued)

As bad sprogs have no bones they have to be pumped up regularly with SPROG GEL.

SLURP

SPROG GEL

SPLOP

① Squidgy gel gland in palm of hand is pressed by fingers

② Gel is squidged into fatter part of arm, causing thinner part to move

③ Horrid sweat gland makes nasty smell during action

Central Computer or Brain

Located inside the head, the 'brain' controls the whole body.
DO NOT attempt 'Home Mechanics' or brain swapping…

because a 'bad' sprog brain in a 'good'
sprog can have dreadful side effects!

Wiring
(or How the Brain Sends Messages to the Body)

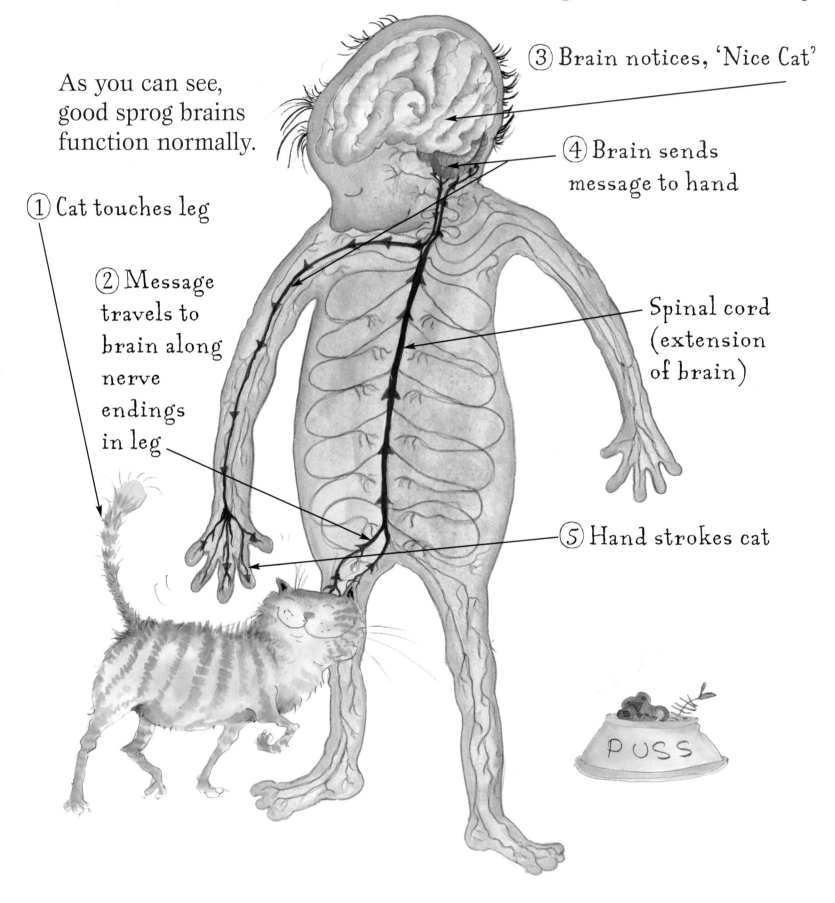

As you can see, good sprog brains function normally.

③ Brain notices, 'Nice Cat'

④ Brain sends message to hand

① Cat touches leg

② Message travels to brain along nerve endings in leg

Spinal cord (extension of brain)

⑤ Hand strokes cat

PUSS

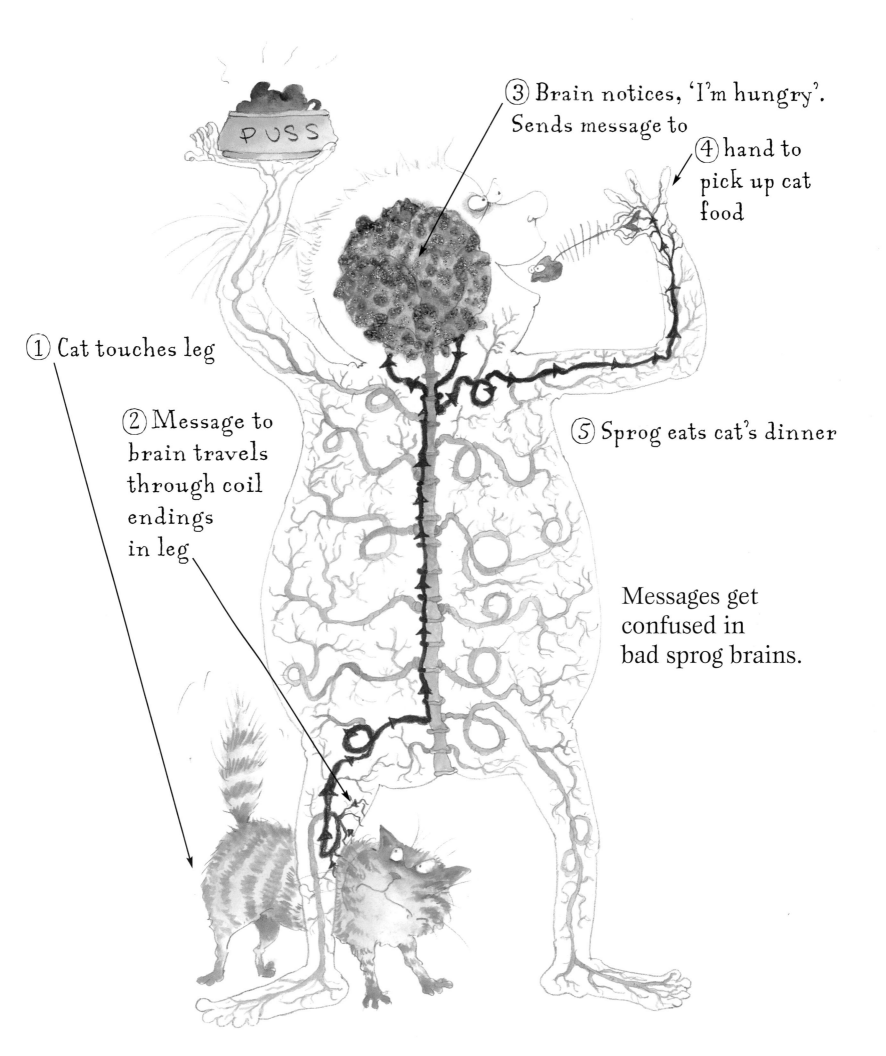

Headlights
(or How Sprogs See)

Blown-up cross section of a good sprog headlight or eye.

④ Image of Mum appears upside down on back of eye

Lens

② Rays of light from Mum

① Mum

⑤ Nerve endings send message to brain

Back of eye or 'retina'

③ Rays of light cross over

Hole in eye or 'pupil'

Coloured part of eye or 'iris'

⑥ Brain says, 'Turn Mum's image the right way up'

⑦ Sprog sees Mum

Blown-up cross section of a bad sprog headlight or eye.

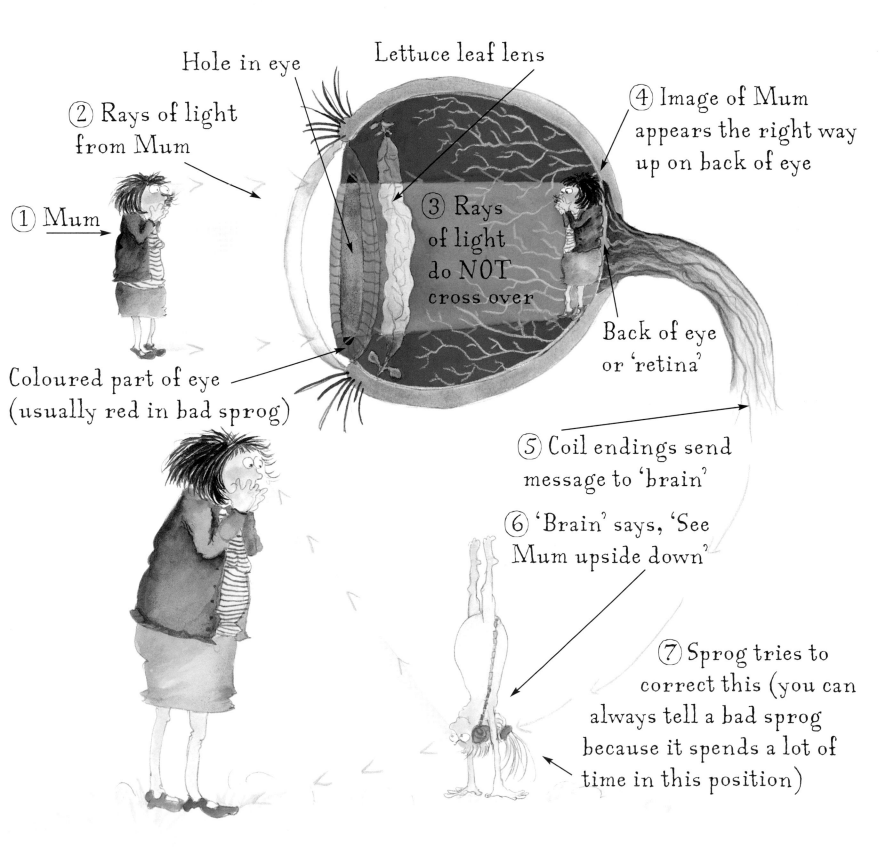

Hole in eye

Lettuce leaf lens

② Rays of light from Mum

④ Image of Mum appears the right way up on back of eye

① Mum

③ Rays of light do NOT cross over

Coloured part of eye (usually red in bad sprog)

Back of eye or 'retina'

⑤ Coil endings send message to 'brain'

⑥ 'Brain' says, 'See Mum upside down'

⑦ Sprog tries to correct this (you can always tell a bad sprog because it spends a lot of time in this position)

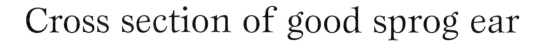

Cross section of good sprog ear

This part of the ear
controls the balance

④ Sound
wobbles
little
bones

⑥ Message
to brain
about sound

⑤ Bones set liquid
and hairy nerve
endings wiggling

① Sound
goes in...
'TIDY
YOUR
ROOM!'

③ Sound vibrates
on ear drum

② Sound
travels
along a
tube called
the 'canal'

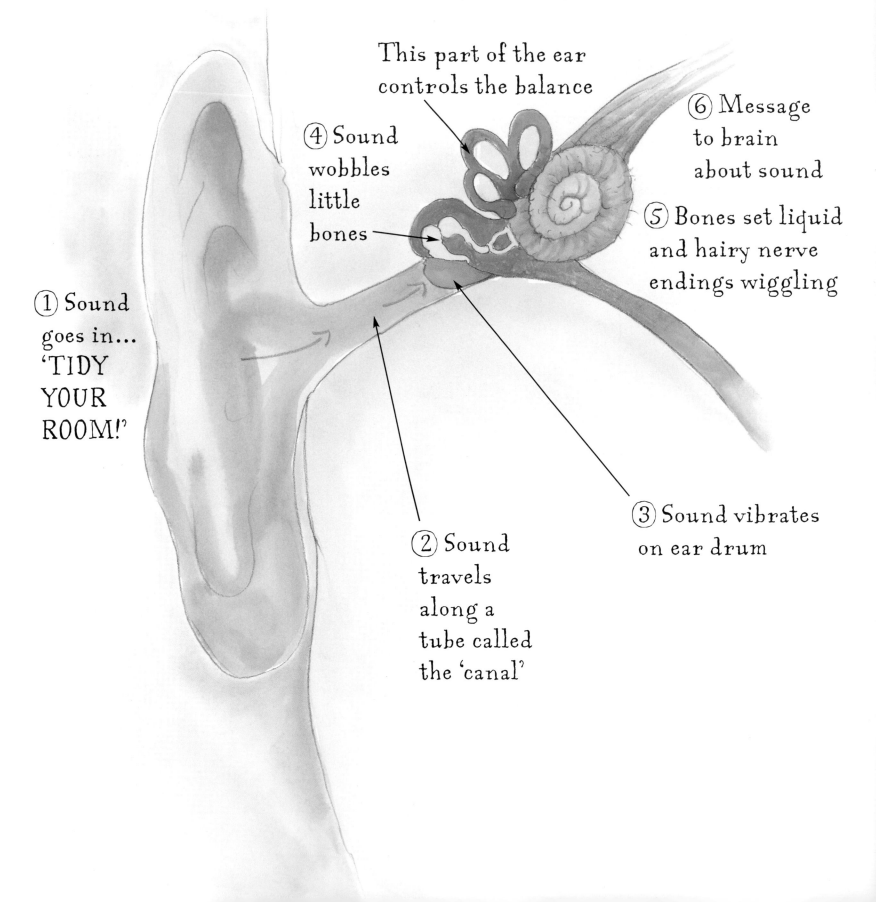

How Sprogs Hear)

Cross section of bad sprog ear

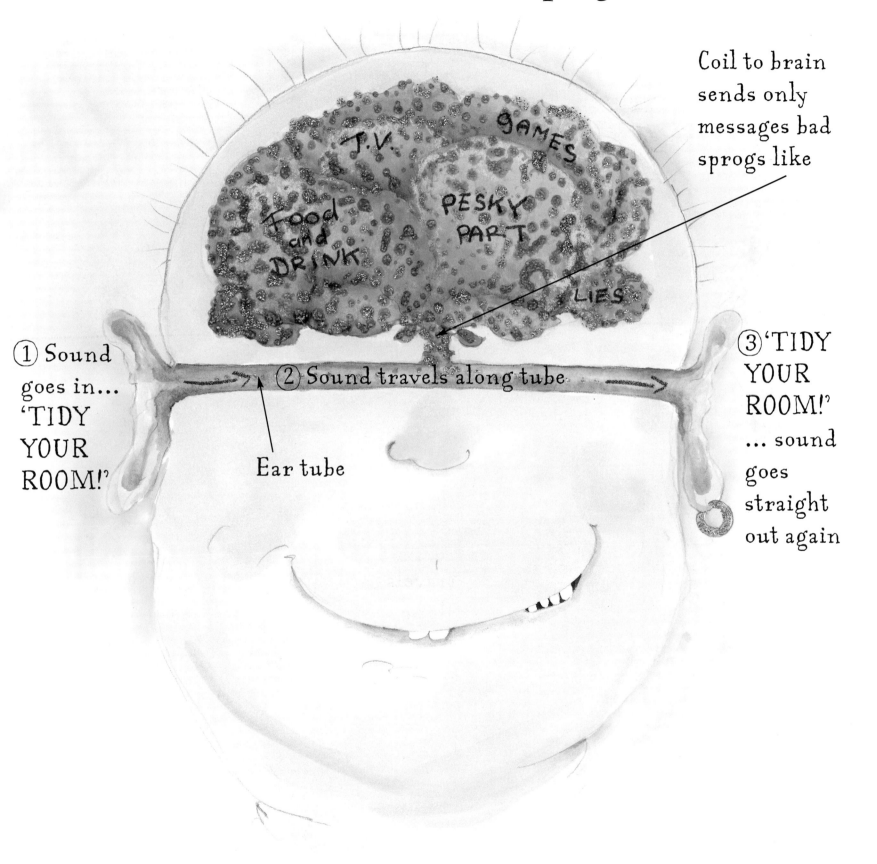

Coil to brain sends only messages bad sprogs like

① Sound goes in... 'TIDY YOUR ROOM!'

② Sound travels along tube

③ 'TIDY YOUR ROOM!' ... sound goes straight out again

Ear tube

General Maintenance
(or How to Make Your Sprog Last)

Achoo

① Do not leave a good sprog out in the rain

② Change nappy and wash regularly

③ Store in a safe, warm place at night

① Do leave bad sprogs out in the rain as they like to rust

② Do not attempt to wash or change nappy

③ Store in a safe place at night

For a
good sprog
call an
ambulance.

Emergency Breakdown

Not much
you can do in
the case of a
bad one.

Helpful Hints
for Future Owners

For Georgie – a good sprog?

THE SPROG OWNER'S MANUAL
A RED FOX BOOK 0 099 44765 7

First published in Great Britain by Jonathan Cape,
an imprint of Random House Children's Books

Jonathan Cape edition published 2004
Red Fox edition published 2005

1 3 5 7 9 10 8 6 4 2

Copyright © Babette Cole, 2004

The right of Babette Cole to be identified as the author and illustrator
of this work has been asserted in accordance with the
Copyright, Designs and Patents Act 1988.

Red Fox Books are published by Random House Children's Books,
61–63 Uxbridge Road, London W5 5SA,
a division of The Random House Group Ltd,
in Australia by Random House Australia (Pty) Ltd,
20 Alfred Street, Milsons Point, Sydney, NSW 2061, Australia,
in New Zealand by Random House New Zealand Ltd,
18 Poland Road, Glenfield, Auckland 10, New Zealand,
and in South Africa by Random House (Pty) Ltd,
Endulini, 5A Jubilee Road, Parktown 2193, South Africa

THE RANDOM HOUSE GROUP Limited Reg. No. 954009
www.**kidsatrandomhouse**.co.uk

A CIP catalogue record for this book is available from the British Library.

Printed in Singapore

More books by the brilliant Babette Cole:

Animals Scare Me Stiff

Dr Dog

Drop Dead

Hair in Funny Places

Mummy Laid an Egg!

Mummy Never Told Me

The Hairy Book

The Silly Book

The Slimy Book

The Smelly Book

The Silly Slimy Smelly Hairy Book

Truelove

Two of Everything